Hypotheticus and His Calculatorium

Written by Quentin Flynn

Illustrated by Ian Forss

Contents

Meet the Characters

Mephalonius

A famous ancient Greek poet.

A Farmer

An ancient Greek lemon farmer.

Hypotheticus

An ancient Greek inventor.

Athenia

Hypotheticus's ancient Greek daughter.

Dear Reader

Imagine what our world would be like if we'd found out how to use electricity thousands of years ago. Here's a fun story about an ancient Greek inventor and his daughter, who may well have had the brightest idea ever!

Quentin Flynn
Author

Spakalis

1. Hypotheticus and Athenia's house
2. The road to Spakalis

Chapter Alpha

I am Mephalonius, the most famous poet in Greece. I write my poetry under an olive tree.

In spring, I can be inspired by the white flower buds overhead.

In summer, I can daydream in the shade of an olive tree's silvery green leaves.

In autumn, I can snooze against its gnarled and twisted trunk.

The Famous Olive Diamante of Mephalonius

Olives
Warm, plentiful
Inspiring, dreaming, snoozing
Petals, breeze, fruit, leaves
Ripening, darkening, softening
Shiny, purple
Pip.

But in winter, that's when the trouble starts.

Olives! Hundreds of them!

At first, they drop off the branches, one at a time – usually when you've just thought of a great word to rhyme with "Hercules".

The Sadly Incomplete Limerick of Mephalonius

There once was a man called Hercules
Who looked like he had …

Splat! Oh dear!

By the time you've wiped the purple olive stain off your robe, you've forgotten what the word was!

There once was a man called Hercules
Who looked like he had …
knocking knees?

No, wait, that doesn't sound right. Splat! Splat!

There once was a man called Hercules
Who looked like he had … itchy fleas.

No, I'm sure that wasn't it, either. Splat! Splat!

That's why, in winter, I leave my olive tree. I roll up my scrolls, pack away my pens and set off on a holiday.

2 Chapter Beta

My friend Hypotheticus is an inventor. He lives in the next village, Spakalis, with his daughter, Athenia. When the first cold winds of winter started to blow, and the first olives began to drop, I decided to visit.

Insects buzzed and birds chirped as I went along the stony road towards Spakalis. But before long, I noticed something very strange.

"What is that lovely smell?" I said to myself.

At that very moment, a farmer and his donkey came around the corner. They had a cart laden with lemons.

"Lemons!" I said. "That's what I can smell!"

The Haiku of a Thousand
Citrus Fruits

Like captured sunshine
Small orbs of golden fragrance
The lemons ripen!

The farmer waved, and I waved back. The cart creaked to a stop.

"*Ou'le*," said the farmer. "Who are you and where are you going?"

"*Ou'le*," I replied. "I am Mephalonius, the most famous poet in Greece.

I am going to stay with my friend Hypotheticus."

The farmer's eyes lit up.

"Mephalonius?" he said. "I've read your poems! Climb on board, and I'll take you to Hypotheticus. I'm taking these lemons to him!"

"Really?" I said. "I didn't know Hypotheticus liked lemons."

"Oh, yes," said the farmer. "Hypotheticus has bought every lemon around. He has thousands in his backyard. The whole village smells like lemons!"

I was curious. I wondered what fantastic idea my friend was working on this winter!

3 Chapter Gamma

Spakalis was a fine village, built on a steep hill. The farmer and his donkey picked their way down the hill, and stopped outside the house where Hypotheticus lived. While they went to unload their lemons, I went to find my friend.

I found him in the garden with Athenia.

"*Ou'le*, Mephalonius!" said my friend, with a smile. "How are you?"

"*Ou'le*, Hypotheticus! *Ou'le*, Athenia!" I replied. "I am well! But what about you both? By the looks of your yard, you have the world's worst colds.

“Are you making the world’s biggest hot lemon drink?”

Athenia laughed. “Those lemons are not for us, Uncle Mephalonius. They are for something much more important.”

“You must come and see my invention,” whispered Hypotheticus excitedly. “I am working on a maths machine that will change the way that humans work, play and swap ideas!”

“Goodness!” I said. “All that, and it is lemon-flavoured as well?”

The Cinquain of Possibilities

Inventions
Clever, mysterious
Ideas that open
Doors to the future
Perhaps!

Hypotheticus and Athenia led me across the pebbles to a wooden door in the steep hillside. Behind it was a cave, carved into the rock. This was where the old stables used to be. Hypotheticus liked to keep his newest, most secret inventions hidden in his cave, where curious eyes could not see them.

Hypotheticus dragged open the door, and my mouth dropped. I stared in amazement. I had never seen anything like this before!

4 Chapter Delta

At first glance, the old stable cave looked as if it were home to a thousand glowworms, hanging from every rock. There was a smell of warm lemons, and I could make out the shapes of cogs, wheels and levers.

Then I saw the lights were not glowworms. I peered at the roof of the cave. The light was coming from fine strands of thread strung between metal wires.

The Illumination Rhyme

A glow worm dangles, and sparkles with life.
A filament glows with light.
A cave full of thoughts transformed into threads
Is a rare and wondrous sight.

"Silk from the cocoons of the Spakalis lesser-spotted cabbage moth," explained Hypotheticus. "You won't find them anywhere else in Greece."

Athenia could barely contain her excitement. "Isn't it fan-tab-ularious?" she said.

Unusually, for a poet, I was lost for words.

"It's very … very pretty," I said.

Hypotheticus and Athenia laughed.

"It's not supposed to be pretty!" said Hypotheticus. "It's a machine!"

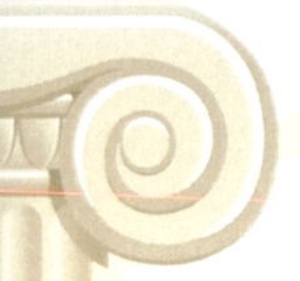

"But what does it do?" I asked.

Hypotheticus and Athenia looked at each other.

"It is the world's first lemon-powered, automatic thinking machine," explained Athenia.

"I call it my calculatorium!" beamed Hypotheticus proudly.

I stared at them both. A thinking machine? I shook my head. Obviously the juice of all these lemons had pickled their brains!

A Not-So-Nonsense Poem

Hypothetically speaking, could it be true?
Was this a machine that thunk?
Could it be a machine that worked like a brain,
Or was it a great pile of junk!
A thinkery, thoughtery, flickery thing
Aglow in the roof of a cave!
Will it ever feel wonder or joy or hope?
Will it ever feel sad or brave?
A thunkering, clunkering thinkery thing
That does what it's told to do,
Is it really so different from donkeys or dogs,
Or from humans, like me or like you?

5 Chapter Epsilon

"Think of a number," said Hypotheticus.

"Three," I said.

"And what is three times forty-seven?" asked Hypotheticus.

I raised my eyebrows. "I don't know," I said. "I only have ten fingers to work with. It will take me a minute or two."

"AHA!" cried Hypotheticus. He pulled some levers with numbers on them, and cogs and wheels started to grind.

A low hum came from a pile of lemons. Zinc and copper wires stuck in the lemons coiled up to the roof, and suddenly a group of mechanical

glowworms shaped like an abacus flicked on and off.

"One hundred and forty-one," declared Hypotheticus confidently, pointing at the roof.

I was amazed. I hadn't even managed to get past one times forty-seven, and Hypotheticus's calculatorium had already figured out the answer.

"If you put zinc and copper into a lemon, a tiny flow of energy comes out," explained Hypotheticus. "I call this energy 'lemonicity'. And with enough lemonicity, I can make my threads of moth silk glow!"

I was astounded.

Athenia went on excitedly, "By running lemonicity through glowing silks in the right order, our calculatorium can figure out answers to mathematical problems. It can think for itself!"

I looked at them both. There was nothing pickled about their brains. They had indeed invented a thinking machine!

Suddenly, the cave was plunged into inky darkness.

"Oops," said Hypotheticus. "Power cut."

A Limerick of Technological Failure

There once was a man in whose stables
Was an engine that worked out "times tables"
But its work was cut short
When it no longer thought.
It had run out of juice in its cables!

6 Chapter Zeta

We all headed out into the sunshine, and pulled the door to the cave closed. We walked back to Hypotheticus's shed, talking excitedly.

"That's my only problem," he said. "The lemons don't last long and there's hardly a tree with any lemons left on it in Spakalis."

"What will you do?" I asked.

"We'll have to shut the calculatorium down until next winter," said Athenia glumly.

"But I believe that one day," said Hypotheticus, "there will be huge power stations, powered by lemons. They will produce enough lemonicity for everyone in a village to use. Why, every house in Greece could have a calculatorium! One day, we might even invent a calculatorium small enough to fit in a donkey cart. Then kids could take their own portable calculatoriums to school and solve their maths problems."

“What a wonderful world that would be!” I said.

“Lemonicity could be used to power talking machines, and seeing machines, and writing machines,” said Athenia enthusiastically.

“And washing machines and cooking machines!” said Hypotheticus.

Suddenly, with a jolt of alarm, I wondered if my days as a poet, sitting under a gnarled and twisted olive tree, watching the white buds blossom, might be at an end.

"What about machines to write poems and stories?" I said. "Could you invent a lemonicity-powered machine to do that?"

Hypotheticus and Athenia looked at each other, and frowned.

"Probably not," said Hypotheticus. "I'm sure there are some human skills that just can't be replaced by machines."

We sat silently for a while, each of us thinking about what the future might be like, when lemonicity was available to everyone.

"Well, that's not so bad," I said. "It's nice to know that there are some things that people will always do better than a calculatorium!"

A Mephalonical Sestet about Ideas before Their Time

A Greek called Hypotheticus, of whom you won't
have heard;

Invented a machine which made him history's
first nerd;

His splendid lemon-powered mathematical machine

Was the first calculatorium the world had ever seen.

But poor old Hypotheticus could never make much
loot ...

Because Greece could only ever grow

a set amount of fruit!

THE END